Solomon
Crocodile

For Colin x

Copyright © 2011 by Catherine Rayner
All rights reserved
First published in Great Britain by Macmillan Children's Books, 2011
Printed in January 2011 in Belgium by Proost, Turnhout
First American edition, 2011
1 3 5 7 9 10 8 6 4 2

mackids.com

Library of Congress Cataloging-in-Publication Data
Rayner, Catherine.
    Solomon Crocodile / Catherine Rayner. — 1st American ed.
        p.   cm.
    "First published in Great Britain by Macmillan Children's Books, 2011."
    Audience: Ages 2–6.
    Summary: Solomon Crocodile's rough play prevents him from making friends
down by the river until a stranger comes stomping through the reeds!
    ISBN: 978-0-374-38064-9 (hardcover)
    1. Crocodiles—Juvenile fiction.   2. Friendship—Juvenile fiction.
3. Play—Juvenile fiction.   4. Picture books for children.   [1. Crocodiles—Fiction.
2. Friendship—Fiction.   3. Play—Fiction.]   I. Title.

PZ7.R2297So 2011
823.92—dc22
[[E]]

                                                                                2010045855

Catherine Rayner

Solomon Crocodile

FARRAR STRAUS GIROUX

NEW YORK

All is peaceful on the banks of the river. Everyone is relaxing in the morning sun, until...

Uh-oh, here comes trouble!

Solomon splats and slops
through the mud to make
the frogs jump.

But the frogs croak,
"Go away, Solomon. You're
nothing but a pest."

So Solomon shakes
the bulrushes and
bugs the dragonflies.

But the dragonflies sing, "Go away, Solomon. You're nothing but a nuisance."

Solomon decides to **stalk** the storks.
They get in such a flap!

"Go away, Solomon," the storks squawk. "You're nothing but a pain."

Out of the corner of his eye,
Solomon spies the biggest
hippo in the river.

This could be the best
fun yet, he thinks.

Solomon charges!

But ...

"SOLOMON," roars the biggest hippo, "GO AWAY! YOU'RE NOTHING BUT TROUBLE!"

Poor Solomon.
No one wants to play.

But then Solomon hears a noise...

Somebody is making the frogs jump.

Somebody is bugging the dragonflies.

And **somebody** has the storks in a flap...

but it is NOT Solomon.

Somebody

is getting nearer...

and nearer...

Uh-oh, here comes . . .

DOUBLE TROUBLE!